A patch of spring sunshine is a pleasant place to read.

"Why does Dave keep looking at me like that?" asked Kate's dad.

"Because you have his chair, Daddy, just where it's warm," said Kate.

For Dee

"All dogs's good dogs."
Jack Biggs, dog owner

WALKER BOOKS
AND SUBSIDIARIES
LONDON · BOSTON · SYDNEY · AUCKLAND

First published 2007 by Walker Books Ltd
87 Vauxhall Walk, London SE11 5HJ

10 9 8 7 6 5 4 3 2 1

Text and illustrations © 2007 Blackbird Design Pty Ltd

The right of Bob Graham to be identified as author/illustrator
of this work has been asserted by him in accordance with the
Copyright, Designs and Patents Act 1988

This book has been typeset in Bulmer

Printed in Singapore

British Library Cataloguing in Publication Data: a catalogue record for this book is available from the British Library

ISBN 978-1-4063-0338-4

www.walkerbooks.co.uk

"The Trouble With DOGS!"

Bob Graham

"The trouble with dogs," said Dad,
"is that they take over your life.
   Run the show."

"What show?" Kate asked,
   then straightaway forgot her question.
"Look," she said, "when I rub Rosy like this
   … her foot scratches like this."

"Interesting," said Dad.
"Hmm," said Mum.
   And they all gazed at Rosy,
   brought home from the
   Rescue Centre eight months back,
   in love and admiration.

While Rosy was large and soft,

comfortable to lie on as an old sofa and endlessly patient …

Dave was small and wild. He slipped and he slid,

he leapt and he skittered. "Take-me-as-you-find-me, don't-care Dave."

"He's so … exuberant!" said Dad.

"What's that?" asked Kate.

"Excited," said Dad.

"Joyful," added Mum.

And they all gazed at Dave,

brought home along with Rosy.

"Full of the joys of spring!" said Mum.

Spring turned to summer
and Dave was still … well … Dave!

In the park, he cut a picnic party
clean in two and ran right down
the middle of the flowerbeds,
just to show it could be done.
"Dave needs a firmer hand," said Mum,
"someone to tell him No."

They all looked at Dad.
"No, Dave," he said.
"No, Dave," Mum called a little louder.
"No, Dave!" said Kate,
as Dave jumped up to lick her on the nose.

Summer drew to a close,
but there was still no
change in Dave.

He often tied Kate in knots,
left small puddles on
the kitchen floor

and pulled holes in
the tights of her school friends.

Then one day he jumped uninvited onto a guest's lap
and ate a cupcake straight off her plate.

"We need help!" said Dad.

Mum went to the phone book.

"Look," she said.

PUP BREAKERS

We Tame Troublesome Beasts

For barkers, biters, breakers and bumpers, post-sniffers,
leaping lead-tanglers and small dogs who smell
nameless spots on the grass and won't move...

We can take the pounce from your pup,
the bounce from your bunny
or the song from your cage bird.

Specially for owners so meek and mild they can't
say "Boo!" to a grasshopper.

Telephone: 1621161625

"That's us!" said Dad.

"Let's call them," said Mum.

Next day, there stood
the Brigadier at 9 a.m. sharp.
"What seems to be the
problem?" he asked.
They all looked at Dave,
a fresh garden flower
hanging from his mouth.

"That dog needs lessons,"
said the Brigadier. "Right now.
Lesson one … is just one word."
A bird twittered nervously.
"One simple little word.

No!"

It knocked the breath
out of all of them.
Dave dropped the flower,
wet and glistening,
to the path.

"Head up, chin in, chest out,
back straight," barked the Brigadier.
"Lesson two …

here!"

"Who … me?" asked Mum.
"No, madam, the pup,"
replied the Brigadier.
"Oh, you mean Dave!" said Mum.

"David, here!"

"Lesson three," the Brigadier went on. "The slip chain. Threaded just so and placed carefully around the neck, it will enable you (with a short sharp jerk) to control your animal.

Ready, David?"

Dave did heel work,

lead work

and sit work.

He trotted,

he waited  and he came.

But no one had the heart for
a "short sharp jerk" on that chain.

At last the Brigadier said,
"We're finished for today.
I'll be back next week
to polish off the rough edges."
He clicked the gate shut
like a trap, while Rosy attended
to some tiny creature deep in
a crease on the inside of her leg.

"What rough edges?" asked Kate.
"Dave has nothing but soft
and squashy bits."
Dad didn't say a word.
Nor did Mum.

In the following days,
a change came
over Dave.

"The trouble is,"
said Dad, "he's
lost his sparkle."

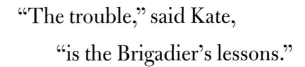

"The trouble is," said Mum,

"he's lost his crackle and fizz."

"The trouble," said Kate,

"is the Brigadier's lessons."

Next week came round and so did the Brigadier.

"Let's make a start!" he shouted.

Dave shivered, but he didn't run away.

Instead he tiptoed slowly forwards...

"He's saying he's glad to see you," said Mum.

"To see *me*?" said the Brigadier.

And then something extraordinary happened.

The man from Pup Breakers smiled.

At least Kate *thought* he smiled.

It was difficult to see under his moustache.

"I think we should have some tea," said Mum.

"And I think we should tell him," Kate said quietly.

"Tell me what?" asked the Brigadier.
Kate blinked, then said, "That Dave
doesn't need lessons any more."
"And why is that, young Kate?"
"Because..." Kate whispered, "because
I think shouting hurts Dave's feelings and
we should always be polite to our dogs."

There was silence.

Then all at once
Dave slipped past Mum.
He slid and he skittered
and he leapt ...

right up on to the Brigadier's
lap and ate the cupcake
straight off his plate.

Then another extraordinary
thing happened.
"Perhaps you're right, Kate,"
the Brigadier said. "Perhaps
we shouldn't shout at our dogs."

He patted Dave's head.
"You're a cute little fella,"
he whispered.
"Share the crumbs with Rosy."
And then he left.

"The *real* trouble with dogs," said Dad
the next day, "is that their ears are
so silky. If you lay Dave's ears across
your knees, and stroke them like this …
have you ever done that?"

"Heaps," nodded Kate.

Dave wagged his tail.

"Lots," added Mum.

Rosy's stomach rumbled.

She fell asleep and snored.

By the following spring, Kate has grown a little more.

"Just move the chairs, Daddy," she says.

"Brilliant idea, Kate!" says Dad. And the sun now warms them both.